Here's what kids and grown-ups have to say about the Magic Tree House® books:

"Oh, man . . . the Magic Tree House series is really exciting!"
—Christina

"I like the Magic Tree House series. I stay up all night reading them. Even on school nights!"
—Peter

"Jack and Annie have opened a door to a world of literacy that I know will continue throughout the lives of my students."
—Deborah H.

"As a librarian, I have seen many happy young readers coming into the library to check out the next Magic Tree House book in the series."
—Lynne H.

Magic Tree House®

For a list of Magic Tree House® Merlin Missions and other Magic Tree House® titles, visit MagicTreeHouse.com.

USE®

#20 DINGOES AT DINNERTIME

BY MARY POPE OSBORNE

ILLUSTRATED BY SAL MURDOCCA

A STEPPING STONE BOOK™

Random House 🏠 New York

For Ellen Mager,

a great champion of children's literature

Text copyright © 2000 by Mary Pope Osborne
Cover art and interior illustrations copyright © 2000 by Sal Murdocca

Visit us on the Web!
SteppingStonesBooks.com
randomhousekids.com
MagicTreeHouse.com

Educators and librarians, for a variety of teaching tools, visit us at
RHTeachersLibrarians.com

Library of Congress Cataloging-in-Publication Data
Osborne, Mary Pope.
Dingoes at dinnertime / by Mary Pope Osborne ; illustrated by Sal Murdocca.
p. cm. — (Magic tree house ; #20) "A Stepping Stone book."
Summary: The magic tree house whisks Jack and Annie away to Australia, where they must save some animals from a wildfire.
ISBN 978-0-679-89066-9 (trade) — ISBN 978-0-679-99066-6 (lib. bdg.) —
ISBN 978-0-375-89477-0 (ebook)
[1. Magic—Fiction. 2. Space and time—Fiction. 3. Zoology—Australia—Fiction.
4. Animals—Fiction. 5. Australia—Fiction.]
I. Murdocca, Sal, ill. II. Title. III. Series: Osborne, Mary Pope. Magic tree house series ; #20. PZ7.O81167Dg 2000 [Fic]—dc21 99-40598

Printed in the United States of America 61 60 59 58 57

This book has been officially leveled by using the F&P Text Level Gradient™ Leveling System.

Contents

Prologue

One summer day in Frog Creek, Pennsylvania, a mysterious tree house appeared in the woods.

Eight-year-old Jack and his seven-year-old sister, Annie, climbed into the tree house. They found that it was filled with books.

Jack and Annie soon discovered that the tree house was magic. It could take them to the places in the books. All they had to do was point to a picture and wish to go there.

Along the way, Jack and Annie discovered

that the tree house belongs to Morgan le Fay. Morgan is a magical librarian from the time of King Arthur. She travels through time and space, gathering books.

In Magic Tree House Books #5–8, Jack and Annie helped free Morgan from a spell. In Books #9–12, they solved four ancient riddles and became Master Librarians.

In Magic Tree House Books #13–16, Jack and Annie had to save four ancient stories from being lost forever.

In Magic Tree House Books #17–20, Jack and Annie must be given four special gifts to help free an enchanted dog from a spell. They have already received a gift on a trip to the *Titanic*, a gift from the Lakota Indians, and a gift from a forest in India. Now they are about to set out in search of their last gift. . .

1
The Last Gift

Annie sat on the porch steps. She stared down the street at the Frog Creek woods.

"Hey, Jack," she said. "Do you hear it?"

Jack sat next to her. He was reading a book.

"Hear what?" he said.

"Teddy's calling us," said Annie.

"You're kidding," said Jack. But he looked down the street and listened, too.

A faint bark came from the distance.

Arf! Arf!

A big smile crossed Jack's face.

"You hear it!" Annie said.

"Yep," said Jack. "You're right. Time to go."

He stood up and grabbed his backpack.

"Be back soon!" Annie shouted through the screen door.

"Don't be late for dinner!" their dad called.

"We won't!" said Jack.

He and Annie ran down the street and into the Frog Creek woods.

Soon they came to the tallest oak.

There was the magic tree house. A little black nose stuck out the window.

"Hi, silly!" Annie called. "We're coming!"

Arf! came a happy bark.

Annie grabbed the rope ladder and started climbing.

Jack followed her up into the tree house.

A small dog sat in a circle of afternoon sunshine. His tail wagged.

"Hey, Teddy!" said Jack.

Jack and Annie hugged Teddy. And the dog licked both of them.

"Morgan's note is still here," said Annie.

"Yep," said Jack. He knew the note by heart now.

This little dog is under a spell and needs your help. To free him, you must be given four special things:

A gift from a ship lost at sea,
A gift from the prairie blue,
A gift from a forest far away,
A gift from a kangaroo.
Be wise. Be brave. Be careful.

Morgan

Beside the note were the gifts from their first three trips:

1. a pocket watch from the *Titanic*
2. an eagle's feather from the prairie skies
3. a lotus flower from a forest in India

"We just need to get a gift from a kangaroo," said Annie, "and Teddy will be free from his spell."

"We must be going to Australia," said Jack. "That's where kangaroos live."

"Cool," said Annie.

Teddy whined and scratched at a book lying in the corner.

Jack picked it up.

"What'd I tell you?" he said.

He showed the cover to Annie. The title was *Adventure in Australia*.

"Great," said Annie. She looked at Teddy.

"Ready to meet a kangaroo?"

Arf! Arf!

Jack opened the book. He found a page with small pictures of different animals and a big picture of a forest. Jack pointed at the forest.

"I wish we could go there," he said.

The wind started to blow.

The tree house started to spin.

It spun faster and faster.

Then everything was still.

Absolutely still.

2
Sleepyhead

Jack opened his eyes. Glaring hot sunlight flooded into the tree house.

"Neat hats," said Annie.

She and Jack were both wearing hats.

"I think they will protect us from the sun," said Jack.

He and Annie looked out the window. Teddy looked out, too.

The tree house had landed in a scrubby forest filled with droopy plants and dry brown trees.

"Man, this place needs rain," said Jack.

He sat back on his heels and looked at the picture of where they had landed in the Australia book.

He read:

> Australia's forests go through times of
> drought (say DROWT). A drought is a
> long period of time without any rain.
> The same forest can be flooded by
> heavy rains at other times of the year.

Jack pulled out his notebook and wrote:

drought = no rain

"Hey, Jack," said Annie. "Doesn't it smell like a cookout?"

Jack sniffed the air. It *did* smell like a cookout.

Jack looked out the window. A wisp of

smoke floated above some trees in the distance.

"Maybe people are camping over there," Jack said.

"Let's go see," said Annie.

Jack put his notebook and the Australia book into his backpack.

"Put Teddy in there, too," said Annie.

Jack slipped the little dog into the pack. Then he followed Annie down the ladder.

When they stepped onto the ground, the hot wind nearly blew their hats off.

"The campers must be over there," said Annie.

She pointed at the smoke in the blue sky. They started walking across a sun-baked clearing.

They passed bushes and scrawny trees. Lizards ran over the dry, cracked ground.

Arf! Arf! Teddy barked from Jack's pack.

"Whoa!" said Jack.

A pair of huge, funny-looking birds walked out from behind a bush.

They were taller than Jack. They had fat bodies, long, skinny legs, and long, skinny necks.

"Who are *you?*" Annie asked the strange pair.

Jack opened his pack and took out the Australia book. He found a picture of the birds.

"They're emus," he said. He read aloud:

> **The emu (say EE-myoo) is a
> large bird that doesn't fly.
> It can run as fast as thirty
> miles per hour.**

"Wow, that's fast," said Annie.

Arf! Teddy jumped out of Jack's backpack and barked at the strange birds.

The emus gave the little dog a haughty look. Then they turned and walked proudly away.

Jack wrote in his notebook:

<u>Emus</u>
proud birds
don't fly

"Look, a *live* teddy bear!" said Annie.

Jack looked up.

Annie ran to a tree at the edge of the

clearing. The "live teddy bear" was nestled in the fork of the tree.

"Aww, it's so cute!" whispered Annie.

The creature was fast asleep. He had large round ears, a black nose, and a furry body. His feet had long, curved claws.

"It's a koala bear," said Jack.

"Hi, sleepyhead," Annie said to the koala.

She patted his soft fur. He opened his big eyes and looked calmly at her.

Jack found a koala picture in the Australia book. He read:

> The koala is actually not a bear at all. It's a marsupial (say mar-SOUP-ee-ul), like a kangaroo. A marsupial mother carries her babies in a stomach pouch.

"That's neat," said Annie.

14

Jack kept reading:

> **Koalas mostly eat the leaves of gum trees, so cutting down gum trees to clear land has hurt them. Wildfires are also a threat. Koalas are slow-moving and can't escape the smoke and flames.**

Jack pulled out his notebook and wrote:

wildfires are a threat to koalas

"What's wrong, sleepyhead?" Annie asked the koala. "Don't you feel well?"

"Don't worry," said Jack. "Listen to this—"
He read more from the book:

> **Koalas, like kangaroos, are active at night and sleep during the day, when the sun is hot. The name "koala"**

means "no drink," because koalas
rarely drink water. They get moisture
from the leaves they eat.

Jack licked his lips. His mouth felt dry.

"Speaking of water," he said, "I'm thirsty."

"Me, too," said Annie.

Teddy was panting, as if he was thirsty, also.

"Let's find those campers," said Jack, sighing. "Maybe they can give us some water."

Jack put Teddy back into his pack. He tucked the book under his arm, in case he needed to look something up.

They began walking again. Suddenly, there was a loud, harsh cackle.

"Yikes," said Annie.

"What was *that?*" said Jack.

3
Big Foot

The loud cry rang again through the dry air.

Teddy barked.

Jack and Annie turned around in the clearing. It was hard to tell where the sound was coming from.

The terrible cackle came again.

"There!" said Annie.

She pointed at a bird in a gum tree. The bird had brown feathers and a large head with a long beak.

It stared down at Jack and Annie. Then it let out another cackle.

"Weird," said Jack.

He found the bird in his book and read:

> The kookaburra (say KOOK-uh-burr-uh) is the best-known bird of Australia. There is even a popular song about it. The kookaburra is also called the "laughing donkey." This is because the strange sound it makes reminds people of a braying donkey.

"I know that song!" said Annie. She began singing:

"Kookaburra sits on the old gum tree-ee.
Merry, merry king of the bush is he-ee . . ."

Jack wrote in his notebook:

kookaburra—a big kook

Annie stopped singing. "Hey," she said. "There's another weird thing."

"Where?" said Jack.

Annie pointed to a big bluish tan lump lying in a shallow, dusty hole.

"Is it alive?" said Jack.

They stepped closer to the big lump.

"It looks like it's breathing," said Annie.

The lump was an animal lying on its back. Its paws were crossed over its chest.

It had huge feet, large ears, a face like a

deer's, and a very long tail. It also had a *very* fat stomach.

Just then, a small head peered out of its stomach.

"Whoa!" said Jack.

"Oh, wow! It's a kangaroo with her baby in her pouch!" said Annie.

"Great!" said Jack. "Remember, we have to get a gift from a kangaroo!"

Their voices woke the kangaroo. The animal jumped up from her shallow bed.

She glared at Jack and Annie. Her baby peeked out of her pouch.

The mother kangaroo gave an angry stamp.

"Oh, we're sorry!" Annie said. "We didn't mean to wake you up."

The kangaroo eyed Annie curiously. Then she took a giant hop toward her.

Copying the kangaroo, Annie hopped toward the big animal.

The kangaroo hopped again.

Annie hopped.

The kangaroo and Annie began hopping around each other. They looked as if they were dancing.

Jack couldn't believe how graceful the kangaroo was. She seemed to fly through the air, then land as softly as a butterfly.

He looked up "kangaroo" in his book and read:

> The kangaroo is the most famous of the marsupials. The female carries her baby, known as a "joey," in her pouch. Scientists call the kangaroo a "macropod," which means "big foot." And big feet help a kangaroo hop higher than any other animal in the world. With a running leap, a large kangaroo can jump over a school bus.

"Forget the hopping contest, Annie," Jack called. "She can out-hop you by a mile."

He pulled out his notebook and wrote:

The kangaroo began stamping her feet again.

"What's wrong?" said Annie.

The kangaroo froze.

Grrrr! Teddy growled from Jack's backpack.

Some nearby bushes moved.

A moment later, three dogs crept silently into the clearing. They were sand-colored and mean-looking.

Teddy growled once more.

But the dogs crept toward the kangaroo.

Suddenly, the mother kangaroo sprang into the air, away from the dogs.

The dogs chased after her.

"Stop!" cried Annie. "Stop! Leave her alone!"

As the kangaroo jumped, she turned in midair and landed facing a different direction. She then zigzagged over rocks and bushes.

Howling, the wild dogs raced after the kangaroo and her baby.

4

Joey

"Oh, no!" cried Annie. "We have to save her!"

She took off after the dogs.

Arf! Arf! Arf! Teddy barked over Jack's shoulder.

Jack ran after Annie with the book under his arm. He ran over the dry, cracked ground, past scrubby bushes and scattered gum trees.

Jack kept his eye on Annie, running ahead of him. He saw her stop suddenly. She turned and dropped to her knees.

"What happened?" he shouted.

"Come look!" she said.

Jack reached Annie. Beside her in the grass was the baby kangaroo. It was trembling.

"Don't be scared," Annie was saying. Then she looked at Jack. "Where's his mom? Why did she drop him?"

"I don't know," said Jack.

He put his pack on the ground and opened the Australia book. Teddy jumped out of the pack.

The little dog tried to sniff the baby kangaroo.

"Don't scare him, Teddy," Annie said.

Teddy sat back and watched politely.

Jack opened the Australia book and found a picture of a baby kangaroo. He read:

> The biggest enemy of the kangaroo is the dingo, the wild dog of Australia. When a mother kangaroo is chased by dingoes, she may throw her joey out of her pouch. Without the extra weight in her pouch, she can leap faster and farther. She then leads the dingoes away from her baby. If she escapes the dingoes, she returns to the joey.

"Oh, Jack," Annie said sadly. "I hope his mother escapes from the dingoes."

"Me, too," said Jack.

"Hi, Joey," said Annie. She gently patted the baby kangaroo. "He's so soft, Jack."

Jack knelt down and touched the brown fur. It *was* soft, the softest fur he had ever felt.

The shy little kangaroo stared at Jack with big brown eyes and trembled.

"Don't be scared, Joey," Annie said. "Your mom's going to come back for you."

Joey jumped away from Jack and Annie. He hopped toward Jack's pack, which was sitting on the ground.

The baby kangaroo took a giant leap and dived headfirst into the pack! His whole body went inside, but his big feet stuck out. Then he turned himself over and peeked out at Jack and Annie.

They both laughed.

"He thinks your pack is a pouch!" said Annie. "I know. Put it on backward. It will feel like when his mom carries him."

Jack put his Australia book on the ground. Then Annie helped him put the pack on his

chest instead of on his back. The joey was heavy!

"There," Annie said. "You look *just* like a mother kangaroo."

"Oh, brother," said Jack.

But he patted the baby's soft fur.

"Don't worry," he said to Joey. "You can stay in there till your mom gets back."

"Here, Joey, would you like some grass to eat?" asked Annie.

Annie scooped up a handful of grass and gave it to the kangaroo.

He munched the grass, keeping his big eyes on Annie.

"I hope his mom comes back for him soon," she said worriedly.

"Yeah," said Jack.

He looked around the dry forest. There was no sign of the mother kangaroo.

But Jack saw something else.

"Look," he said to Annie.

The wisp of smoke in the sky had turned into a big black cloud. Jack noticed the smell of burning wood was much stronger.

"What are those campers doing?" said Annie. "Are they making a bonfire now or what?"

A feeling of dread came over Jack.

"What if . . ." he said. "What if . . ."

In the distance, a tree suddenly burst into flames.

"We're looking at a *wildfire!*" he said.

5
Wildfire!

"Wildfire?" said Annie.

"The woods are so dry, everything's starting to burn!" said Jack. "We have to get out of here."

"We can't leave Joey," said Annie.

"We'll take him with us!" said Jack.

"But what if his mom comes back for him and he's not here?" said Annie.

"We don't have a choice," said Jack.

Just then, the kookaburra flew through
the sky, cackling.

The emus raced by at top speed.

The air was getting smokier and smokier.
The fire was spreading quickly!

"Come on!" said Jack. "We have to get back to the tree house before it burns down!"

"Which way's the tree house?" said Annie.

"I'm not sure," said Jack.

Smoke hid the treetops. Jack's eyes stung.

"Forget it," he said. "Let's just get away from this smoke. Come on!"

Jack and Teddy turned to go. The baby kangaroo hid his head inside Jack's pack.

"I'll catch up!" said Annie. "I have to get something!"

"*What?*" cried Jack.

But Annie had dashed off in the other direction.

"Come back!" Jack shouted. "Annie!"

Branches cracked and fell from the trees. Smoke billowed everywhere.

Arf! Arf!

"Annie!" Jack cried.

Jack choked on the smoke. He coughed and rubbed his eyes. The air was getting hotter.

He had no choice. He had to run.

Arf! Arf! Teddy barked from somewhere ahead.

"Hurry, Annie!" Jack called helplessly. Then he took off after Teddy.

He stumbled blindly through the brush. All he could do was follow the sound of Teddy's barking. His pack felt heavier and heavier. He held it up with his arms and kept going.

Suddenly, Jack heard Annie calling him.

Jack stopped.

"Here! Here! Here! We're here!" he shouted. "Come on! Follow us!"

Annie appeared through the haze of the hot smoke. She was coughing. Tears streamed from her eyes.

She was carrying the koala!

"Come on!" Jack cried. "Follow Teddy!"

Arf! Arf!

Jack and Annie carried Joey and the koala. They followed Teddy's barking through the smoky, fire-filled forest.

Finally, they came to a giant rock.

Arf! Arf!

Teddy was standing on a ledge. Behind him was the mouth of a cave.

Through the smoke, Jack could barely see the little dog.

Teddy barked again, then vanished inside the cave.

"Follow him!" said Annie.

6
Hand to Hand

Jack and Annie climbed onto the rock ledge and stepped into the cave. The air inside was cleaner and cooler than the air outside.

"I can't see anything," said Jack.

He patted the head of the baby kangaroo.

"Me neither," said Annie.

Arf! Arf!

"I guess we'll have to follow Teddy's bark," said Annie. "Let's hold hands."

She held out her free hand to Jack. Jack

took it. Then he put his other hand out and touched the wall. The joey moved in his pack.

Jack and Annie walked into the darkness.

Arf!

Teddy kept barking, leading them on.

Arf!

Arf!

Arf!

Arf!

Suddenly, Jack felt something thump against his leg. He stopped and gasped.

"What is it?" said Annie.

Arf!

It was Teddy! His tail was wagging and hitting Jack's leg.

"What is it, boy?" Jack asked him.

Teddy let out a howl.

As he howled, an amazing thing happened.

A white line began to glow in the air. The glowing line grew until it looked like a giant snake. Then glowing handprints appeared below the snake.

Jack felt Annie squeeze his hand.

"I think it's painted on the wall," she said.

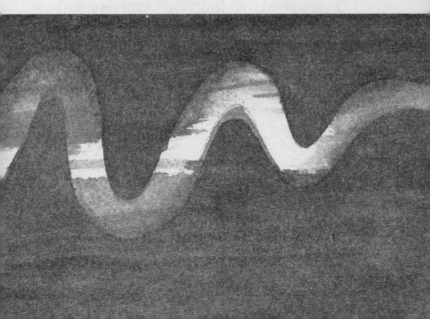

"But what is it?" whispered Jack.

"I don't know," said Annie.

She let go of Jack and put her hand inside one of the painted handprints.

Jack did the same.

Despite the glowing painting, the rock felt smooth and cool. It almost seemed to breathe.

A ghost-like whistling sound came through the darkness. Then a loud boom!

"What's *that?*" Jack quickly took his hand off the wall.

The boom came again.

"It sounded like thunder," said Annie.

Arf! Arf!

"Teddy's leaving!" said Annie.

She grabbed Jack's hand. They turned back the way they had come and followed Teddy's barking again.

Arf!

They followed the little dog until they saw a flash of light.

"Lightning," said Annie. "Lightning and thunder! We're at the front of the cave! Yay!"

Annie pulled Jack toward the mouth of the cave and out, into a pouring rain.

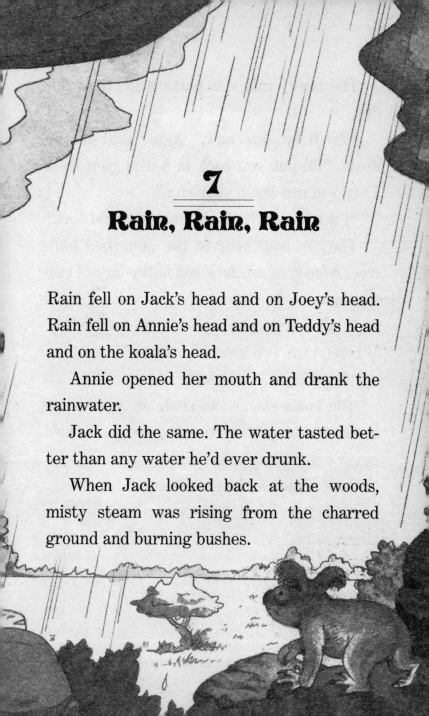

7
Rain, Rain, Rain

Rain fell on Jack's head and on Joey's head. Rain fell on Annie's head and on Teddy's head and on the koala's head.

Annie opened her mouth and drank the rainwater.

Jack did the same. The water tasted better than any water he'd ever drunk.

When Jack looked back at the woods, misty steam was rising from the charred ground and burning bushes.

The heavy rain was putting out the wild-fire.

"You'll be safe now," Annie said to the koala. "I'll put you back in a nice gum tree. Then you can finish your nap."

"I see a tree that's not burned," said Jack.

They walked over to the unburned gum tree. Annie placed the koala in the fork of two branches.

"Go back to sleep now," she said softly. "Pretend the fire was all a dream."

"Good night," said Jack.

The koala seemed to smile at them. Then he closed his eyes and went to sleep, as if he'd never been disturbed at all.

Jack sighed and looked around.

"Man," he said, "we were lucky that a storm came."

Annie smiled.

"It wasn't just luck," she said. "It was magic."

"Magic?" said Jack.

"Yeah . . . the glowing hands and the snake," said Annie. "Somehow they brought the storm."

"That doesn't make sense," said Jack.

Joey stirred in his pack. Suddenly, Jack remembered something.

"Hey, we have to get Joey back to the place where his mom left him," he said. "Or she won't be able to find him."

"Where was that place?" said Annie.

"I don't know," said Jack.

He looked around at the rainy gray forest. Everything looked the same.

"Teddy can find the spot!" said Annie.

Without even a bark, the little dog took off across the wet, muddy ground.

Once again, Jack and Annie followed him. Jack's back was beginning to hurt from carrying Joey.

Arf! Arf!

Jack and Annie caught up with Teddy. He stood over the Australia book! It was wet, but not burned.

"Hurray, we found it!" said Annie.

"That's right!" said Jack. "I left our book in the spot where we found Joey!"

"Once again, Teddy helped us out," said Annie.

She patted the little dog's head.

"Thanks, Teddy," Jack said.

He picked up the Australia book. The cover was wet, but the pages looked okay.

The little kangaroo peeked out of his pack as Jack tucked the book under his arm.

"Don't worry, Joey," Annie said. "We'll stay right here till your mom comes back for you."

If she hasn't already come . . . Jack thought worriedly.

Jack and Annie stood in the rain with Teddy and Joey and waited.

They waited and waited.

The rain turned to a drizzle. Then the drizzle turned to a light sprinkle.

Still, they waited . . .

Jack grew sadder and sadder.

Maybe the mother kangaroo *had* come and left. Or maybe she had been caught by the dingoes. Or maybe she had been killed by the wildfire.

Jack was afraid to look at Annie, afraid to say anything.

"I know what you're thinking," she said finally.

Jack patted Joey's head and sighed.

"Let's wait a little longer," he said. "If she doesn't come back soon, we'll take him home with—"

Arf! Teddy barked softly.

"*Listen*," said Annie.

Jack listened.

The sound was very faint at first. But then it grew louder.

It was a squishy sound. It was a squashy sound. It was the sound of big feet slapping through mud!

8

The Rainbow Serpent

The mother kangaroo bounded out of the trees.

She landed ten feet away from Jack, Annie, Teddy, and Joey.

They all were still for a moment, as if they all were holding their breath.

Then Joey tried to jump out of Jack's backpack.

"Hold on," said Jack.

He put his pack on the ground.

The little kangaroo leaped out.

He leaped again . . . then again . . . and dived headfirst into his mother's pouch!

Joey turned himself over inside the pouch. Then he peeked out at Jack and Annie.

"Yay!" said Jack and Annie together. They laughed and clapped with relief.

"He looks happy to be home," said Annie.

"His mother looks happy, too," said Jack.

The mother kangaroo was gazing down at her joey. She patted his head with her small paws.

Then she looked at Jack and Annie with soft eyes.

"She's saying thank you to us," Annie said.

"You're welcome," Jack said.

"It was no problem," Annie told the kangaroo. "You have a great joey."

The kangaroo gave a little nod. Then she bent over and used a front paw to pick up a small piece of bark from the wet grass.

The kangaroo held the piece of bark out to Jack and Annie.

Jack took it from her.

"Oh, man," he whispered. "It's our *gift from a kangaroo.*"

The kangaroo then sprang into the air. She bounded gracefully away through the charred forest.

"Thanks!" called Jack.

"Bye!" called Annie. "Good luck!"

Arf! Arf! Teddy barked.

The rain stopped as Jack studied the piece of bark. There was a tiny painting on it. It was just like the snake painting in the cave.

"I wonder what the snake means," said Jack.

Jack opened the wet cover of the Australia book. He carefully turned the damp pages. He found a picture of the snake painting.

"Listen," said Jack. He read:

The first people of Australia are called "Aborigines" (say ab-uh-RIJ-uh-neez). They have lived there for 40,000 years. Their myths take place in a time they call "Dreamtime." In Dreamtime, there is a Rainbow Serpent, who sends life-giving rain.

Aborigine artists paint the Rainbow Serpent on cave walls or on pieces of bark. In special ceremonies, they sometimes honor the Rainbow Serpent by painting their handprints on the magic snake.

"See?" said Annie. "That explains everything!"

"Explains what?" said Jack.

"We put our hands on the painting of the Rainbow Serpent," she said. "It was like a special ceremony. So the Rainbow Serpent sent the rain to put out the wildfire."

Arf! Teddy barked.

Jack frowned.

"But it's not a real creature," he said. "It's in *Dream*time. Not *real* time."

Annie smiled.

"Then how do you explain *that?*" she said. She pointed at the sky.

The rain clouds were gone. The sun had come back out.

A rainbow curved across the blue Australian sky.

"Oh, man," whispered Jack. Though the air was warm again, he shivered.

"Teddy led us to the painting," said Annie. "We should thank him."

"How did he know about the Rainbow Serpent in the cave?" Jack asked.

"I told you," said Annie. "He has a touch of magic."

They looked down at the little dog. Teddy tilted his head and seemed to smile.

"Hey, we have all four gifts now!" said Annie.

"Oh, yeah!" said Jack.

"Let's go home and see if Teddy's spell is broken!" said Annie.

Arf! Arf!

Jack put the bark painting and the Australia book in his pack. Then they all headed through the wet, steamy forest in the direction of the tree house.

"I hope the tree house didn't get burned!" he said.

They went past the clearing, past the gum trees and bushes.

The tree house was waiting for them.

"*It's still here!*" said Annie.

She grabbed the rope ladder and started up.

Jack put Teddy in his pack and followed.

Inside the tree house, Teddy wiggled out of the pack. He pawed the Pennsylvania book.

Arf! Arf!

"Okay, okay," said Jack. He pointed at a picture of the Frog Creek woods. "I wish we could go there!"

"Over the rainbow!" said Annie.

And the wind started to blow.

The tree house started to spin.

It spun faster and faster.

Then everything was still.

Absolutely still.

9
What Boy?

"Welcome back," came a soft, lovely voice.

Jack opened his eyes.

It was Morgan! They hadn't seen Morgan in a long time.

"Morgan!" cried Annie.

She threw her arms around the enchantress. Jack jumped up and hugged Morgan, too.

"It's good to see you both," said Morgan.

Arf! Arf!

"And it's good to see *you*, too," Morgan said, smiling at the little dog.

"Look," said Annie. She reached into Jack's pack and pulled out the piece of painted bark. "A gift from a kangaroo."

"We have all four gifts now," said Jack.

"Good work," said Morgan.

She picked up their first gift. It was the pocket watch from the *Titanic*.

"Once upon a time, there was a boy who wasted time," Morgan said. "This watch teaches him that time is very precious. It must be used wisely."

Morgan picked up their second gift, the eagle's feather from the Lakota Indians.

"Sometimes the boy was afraid to stand up for himself," she said. "The eagle's feather teaches him that a small creature can be one of the bravest."

Morgan picked up the lotus flower from the forest in India.

"Sometimes the boy did not respect nature," she said. "This flower teaches him that nature holds many wonders."

Morgan picked up the piece of bark with the painting of the Rainbow Serpent.

"Sometimes the boy didn't want to study other times and places," she said. "This painting teaches him there is mystery, magic, and wisdom in the traditions of ancient peoples."

"What boy?" Jack asked.

"Who are you talking about?" asked Annie.

Morgan didn't answer right away. She placed her hands on Jack's and Annie's shoulders.

"Thank you," she said, "for helping this

boy learn his lessons. Thank you for breaking the spell."

"What boy?" Jack asked again.

Arf! Arf! Arrrrrrrf!

Jack and Annie looked over at Teddy.

Then something magical happened.

In a flutter of time . . .

in the spin of a whirlwind . . .

Teddy was changed.

He was no longer a dog.

He was a *boy*.

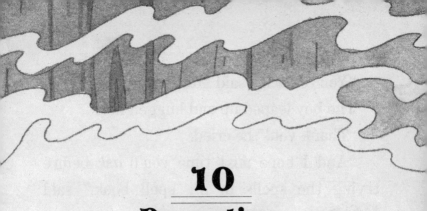

10
Dreamtime

The boy was on the ground on his hands and knees.

"Meet my young helper from Camelot," said Morgan.

The boy glanced up. He had a friendly freckled face and twinkly dark eyes. His hair was the same color that Teddy's fur had been. He looked a bit older than Jack, about ten or so.

"Am I back?" he asked.

"You're back," said Morgan.

The boy leaped up and hugged her.

"Thank you!" he cried.

"And I hope next time you'll *ask* before trying the spells in my spell book," said Morgan.

The boy grinned sheepishly.

"I promise." Then he looked at Jack and Annie. "I accidentally changed myself into a dog," he said.

Annie laughed.

"But at least I got to have exciting adventures as a dog!" he said.

"You were a *great* dog," said Annie. "We liked you as Teddy. What's your real name?"

"If you like, you can keep calling me Teddy," the boy said. "Or how about Ted?"

"Okay, Ted," said Annie.

Jack just nodded. He was still in shock.

"Ted is training to work in my library at Camelot," said Morgan. "He has a rare gift for magic."

"Cool," said Annie.

"You—you helped us a lot, Ted," said Jack, finally finding his voice.

"Oh, no, it was both of *you* who helped me," said Ted. "You helped break the spell. And I found new stories to take home."

"You did?" said Annie.

Ted nodded.

"The story of the *Titanic*, the story of White Buffalo Woman, the story of the wounded tiger, and the story of the Rainbow Serpent," he said. "I'll write them down as soon as I get home. So people can read them in Morgan's library."

"And home is where we must go now, I'm afraid," said Morgan.

"Oh," said Annie sadly. "That's too bad."

"Yeah," said Jack. He was sad, too.

"I know we will meet again someday," said Ted.

"I hope so," said Jack.

"Me, too," said Annie. "Bye!"

She started down the ladder.

Jack pulled on his pack. With a heavy heart, he followed.

When they got to the ground, they looked up.

Morgan and Ted were at the window. They both seemed to glow in the late afternoon light.

"The magic tree house will return for you soon," said Morgan. "I promise."

She waved, and they waved back.

"Good-bye, Jack and Annie," she said.

"Arf!" said Ted.

In a flutter of time . . .

in the spin of a whirlwind . . .

the magic tree house was gone.

For a long moment, Jack and Annie stared at the empty tree.

"Ready for dinner?" Annie asked softly.

Jack nodded.

He felt dazed as they walked silently through the Frog Creek woods.

When they came to their street, the sun was setting. A flock of black birds flew through the silvery pink sky.

Annie broke their silence as they headed for their house.

"We had great adventures with Teddy—I

mean Ted—didn't we?" she said.

"Yeah," said Jack. "It was like . . ." He searched for the right words. "Like . . ."

"Like living in Dreamtime," said Annie.

"Yeah," said Jack. He smiled.

That was *exactly* what it was like.

MORE FACTS FOR YOU AND JACK

1) Australia is the world's smallest and flattest continent. The country of Australia is the only nation in the world to occupy a whole continent. The continent is almost 3 million square miles, or the size of the United States without Alaska and Hawaii.

2) At one time, all the continents on earth were part of one huge land mass. Australia became separated from this mass about 200 million years ago. Because it is a separate continent, its animals have evolved differently from those on other continents.

3) Among the animals that live on Australia are 170 different kinds of marsupials, including koalas, wombats, kangaroos, and wallabies

(which are like kangaroos, only smaller). The only marsupials that live outside Australia are opossums.

4) Kangaroos have been in Australia for 25 million years. For every person in Australia, there are ten kangaroos—and there are almost 19 million people in Australia! A kangaroo hops at about 11 mph but can put on bursts of speed of up to 30 mph.

5) Dingoes were used as hunting dogs by the Aborigines.

6) Koalas feed on gum trees, which are also known as eucalyptus (say yoo-cuh-LIP-tus) trees. People use the oil of the eucalyptus tree in medicines for colds and flu. Eucalyptus also has a strong smell that many people enjoy.

The Rainbow Serpent

In Aborigine myth, the Rainbow Serpent not only brings rain but also helped create the world.

At the beginning of time, the Rainbow Serpent awoke from sleep and pushed through the earth's crust. As it traveled over the empty land, it left behind deep tracks.

The Rainbow Serpent called to the frogs to come out from beneath the earth. It tickled the frogs' bellies, and when they laughed, water poured from their mouths. The water filled the Rainbow Serpent's tracks, making rivers and lakes.

Grass grew. Then all creatures—birds, lizards, snakes, kangaroos, koalas, and dingoes—woke up and took their places on the earth.

Track the facts with Jack and Annie!

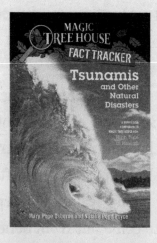

Magic Tree House® Fact Trackers are the must-have,
all-true companions to your favorite
Magic Tree House® adventures!

Here's a special preview of

Magic Tree House® #21

CIVIL WAR ON SUNDAY

Jack and Annie help wounded

soldiers in the time of the

War Between the States. . . .

Excerpt copyright © 2000 by Mary Pope Osborne.
Illustrations copyright © 2000 by Sal Murdocca. Published by Random House
Children's Books, a division of Penguin Random House LLC, New York.

1
A Light in the Woods

Jack looked out his window.

It was a dreary Sunday afternoon. There were dark clouds in the sky.

Thunder rumbled in the distance.

Jack stared down the street at the Frog Creek woods.

When is the magic tree house coming back? he wondered.

"Hey, guess what!" Annie said. She charged into Jack's room. "I saw a light flash in the woods!"

"It was just lightning," said Jack.

"No, it was magic! A swirl of light!" said Annie. "I think the tree house just came back!"

"I'm sure it was just lightning," Jack said. "Didn't you hear the thunder?"

"Yeah," said Annie. "But let's go check anyway."

She started out of Jack's room. Then she peeked back in.

"Bring your backpack, just in case!" she said.

Jack was always glad for a chance to look for the magic tree house. He grabbed his backpack and followed Annie down the stairs.

"Where are you two going?" their mom called.

"Out to play," said Annie.

"Don't go far," said their mom. "And come in if it starts to rain."

"We will," said Jack. "Don't worry."

They slipped out the front door. Then they ran up the street and into the Frog Creek woods.

The woods were dark under the storm clouds. A cool wind shook the leaves.

Soon Jack and Annie came to the tallest oak tree.

"Oh, man," said Jack. "You were right!"

The magic tree house stood out against the gray sky.

"Morgan!" called Annie.

There was no sign of the enchantress.

"Let's go up!" said Jack.

He grabbed the rope ladder and started up. Annie followed.

They climbed into the tree house. It was hard to see in the dim light.

"Look," said Annie.

She pointed to a piece of paper and a book lying on the floor.

Jack picked up the paper. Annie picked up the book.

"Listen," said Jack. He held the paper close to the window and read aloud:

Dear Jack and Annie,

Camelot is in trouble. To save the kingdom, please find these four special kinds of writing for my library:

Something to follow
Something to send
Something to learn
Something to lend

Thank you,
Morgan

"Camelot is in trouble?" said Jack. "What's that mean?"

"I don't know," said Annie. "But we better hurry and find these writings. Let's go look for the first: *Something to follow*."

"I wonder where we should look for it," said Jack. "What's the title of the book you're holding?"

Annie held the book close to the window to read the title.

"Yikes," she said softly. She showed the book to Jack.

On the cover was a painting of a peaceful-looking field and a blue sky. The title said *The Civil War*.

"The Civil War?" said Jack. "Cool."

Annie frowned.

"*Cool?*" she said. "War's not cool."

"It sort of is," Jack said uncomfortably. He knew war was bad. But some parts of it seemed fun, like a game.

"I guess we'll find out," said Annie. She pointed at the cover. "I wish we could go there."

Thunder boomed through the woods.

The wind started to blow.

The tree house started to spin.

It spun faster and faster.

Then everything was still.

Absolutely still.

Magic Tree House®
Super Edition

#1: WORLD AT WAR, 1944

Magic Tree House®
Fact Trackers

DINOSAURS

KNIGHTS AND CASTLES

MUMMIES AND PYRAMIDS

PIRATES

RAIN FORESTS

SPACE

TITANIC

TWISTERS AND OTHER TERRIBLE STORMS

DOLPHINS AND SHARKS

ANCIENT GREECE AND THE OLYMPICS

AMERICAN REVOLUTION

SABERTOOTHS AND THE ICE AGE

PILGRIMS

ANCIENT ROME AND POMPEII

TSUNAMIS AND OTHER NATURAL DISASTERS

POLAR BEARS AND THE ARCTIC

SEA MONSTERS

PENGUINS AND ANTARCTICA

LEONARDO DA VINCI

GHOSTS

LEPRECHAUNS AND IRISH FOLKLORE

RAGS AND RICHES: KIDS IN THE TIME OF
   CHARLES DICKENS

SNAKES AND OTHER REPTILES

DOG HEROES

ABRAHAM LINCOLN

PANDAS AND OTHER ENDANGERED SPECIES

HORSE HEROES

HEROES FOR ALL TIMES

SOCCER

NINJAS AND SAMURAI

CHINA: LAND OF THE EMPEROR'S GREAT
   WALL

SHARKS AND OTHER PREDATORS

VIKINGS

DOGSLEDDING AND EXTREME SPORTS

DRAGONS AND MYTHICAL CREATURES

WORLD WAR II

More Magic Tree House®

GAMES AND PUZZLES FROM THE TREE HOUSE

MAGIC TRICKS FROM THE TREE HOUSE

MY MAGIC TREE HOUSE JOURNAL

MAGIC TREE HOUSE SURVIVAL GUIDE

ANIMAL GAMES AND PUZZLES

MAGIC TREE HOUSE INCREDIBLE FACT BOOK

CALLING ALL ADVENTURERS!

Join the

MAGIC TREE HOUSE®
KIDS' ADVENTURE CLUB

Members receive:

- Exclusive packages delivered throughout the year
- Members-only swag
- A sneak peek at upcoming books
- Access to printables, games, giveaways, and more!

With a parent's help, visit MagicTreeHouse.com to learn more and to sign up!